Birthday Wishes SEAN

by Suzanne Marshall

LiveWellMedia.com

ISBN-13: 978-1544299389
ISBN-10: 1544299389

This book is dedicated to

who is loved very much!

Sean,

the bees are buzzing
with the news
of birthday wishes
just for you.

Sean,

a panda plays a birthday song,
wishing you joy the whole day long!

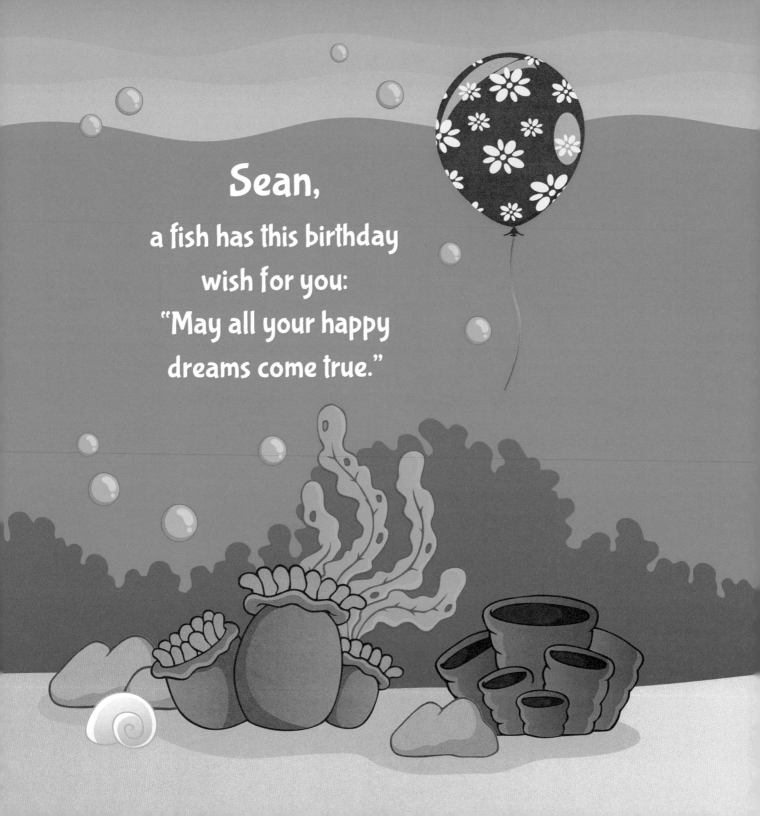

Sean,
a fish has this birthday
wish for you:
"May all your happy
dreams come true."

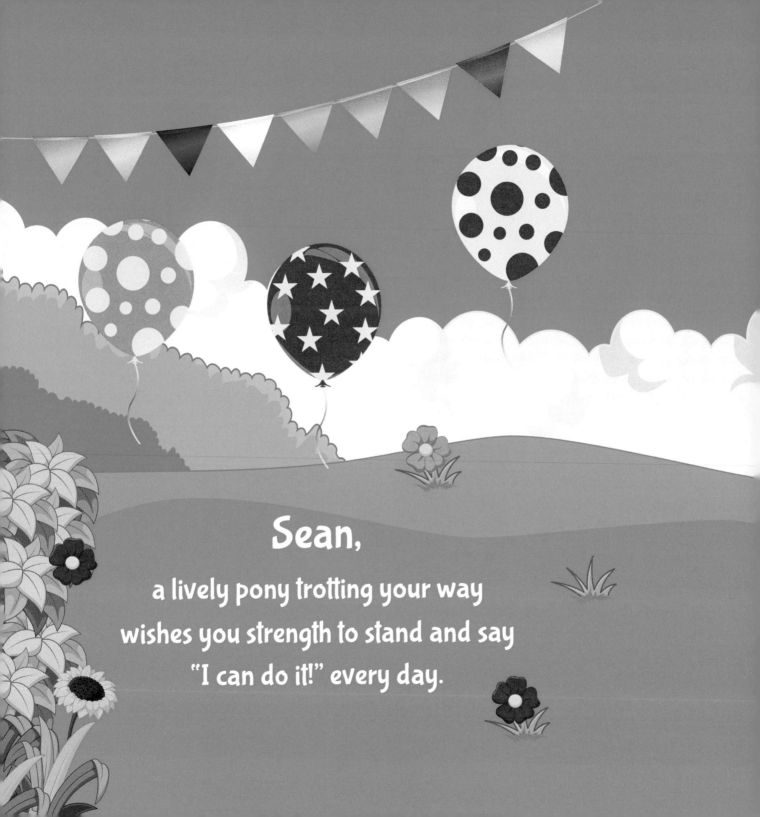

Sean,
a lively pony trotting your way
wishes you strength to stand and say
"I can do it!" every day.

Sean,

a piggy wishes you lots of pluck.
So when you fall, you rise back up.

Sean,

an elephant has this wish for you:
a bright and positive attitude
to fill your heart with gratitude.

HAPPY
BIRTHDAY

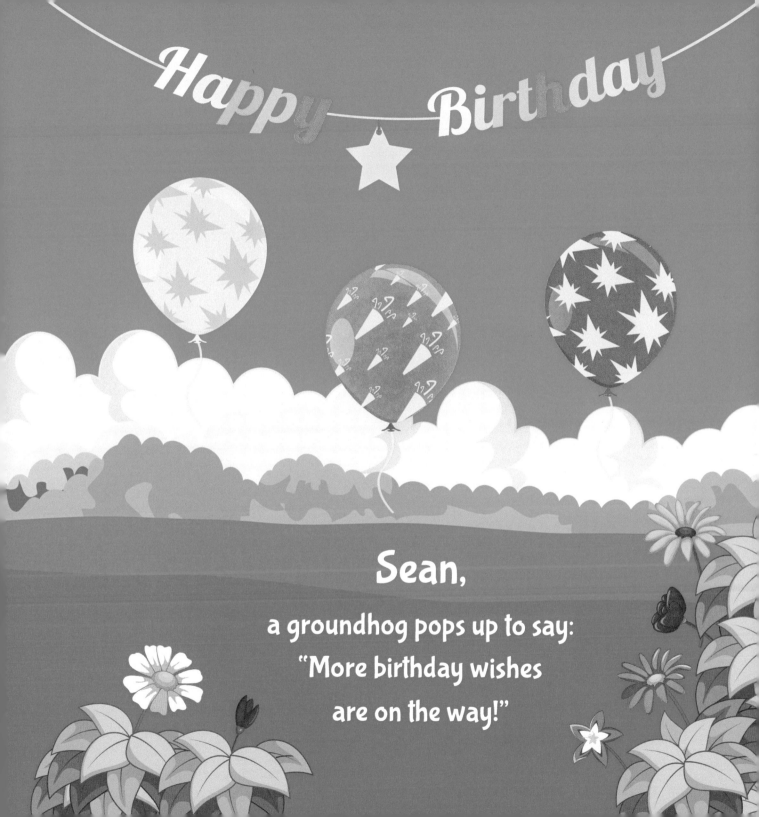

Sean,

a lion wishes you lots of smiles,
since smiles never go out of style.

Sean,

playful monkeys wearing hats
wish you giggles, chuckles and laughs.

Sean,

a lamb makes a wish
that has already come true:
lots and lots of love for you!

Happy
Birthday

A dog and cat exclaim with glee:
"Sean is loved to the utmost degree.
Sean is loved to infinity!"

Sean,

all your friends come out to say:
"Hip, hip, hooray, and happy birthday!
We love you, Sean, every day."

Your birthday love never ends.
So pass it on to family and friends.
Spread birthday love to ALL with cheer.
Spread birthday love throughout the year!

Sean!

Special Thanks

to my parents for their love and support, and to my awesome editorial team: Hannah & Rachel Roeder, and Don Marshall. Artwork has been edited by the author. Original scenes: © Colematt, © Tigatelu, © Bluering (fotosearch.com). Original cat, chicks, dog, fish, groundhog, lamb, lion, panda, pony, tiger: © Dazdraperma (fotosearch.com). Original bee, elephant, monkeys & pig: © Tigatelu (fotosearch.com). Additional images curated from freepik.com.

About the Author

An honors graduate of Smith College, Suzanne Marshall writes to engage and empower children. Her children's books are full of positive affirmations and inspirational quotes. Learn more about Suzanne and her books at: LiveWellMedia.com.

Made in the USA
Monee, IL
17 October 2021

80231372R00021